W

# The Chickens and the Eggs

adapted by Farrah McDoogle

based on the screenplay "Omelet Party" written by Olivier Jean-Marie
and adapted into English by David Gasman

illustrated by Shane L. Johnson

Simon Spotlight
New York    London    Toronto    Sydney    New Delhi

SIMON SPOTLIGHT

An imprint of Simon & Schuster Children's Publishing Division

1230 Avenue of the Americas, New York, New York 10020

This Simon Spotlight edition September 2014

SIMON SPOTLIGHT, READY-TO-READ, and colophon are registered trademarks of Simon & Schuster, Inc.

For information about special discounts for bulk purchases, please contact Simon & Schuster Special Sales at 1-866-506-1949 or business@simonandschuster.com.

The Simon & Schuster Speakers Bureau can bring authors to your live event. For more information or to book an event contact the Simon & Schuster Speakers Bureau at 1-866-248-3049 or visit our website at www.simonspeakers.com.

Manufactured in the United States of America 0814 LAK

2 4 6 8 10 9 7 5 3 1

ISBN 978-1-4814-0043-5 (hc)

ISBN 978-1-4814-0042-8 (pbk)

ISBN 978-1-4814-0044-2 (eBook)

# CONTENTS

# CHAPTER 1:
# THE STRANGE CREATURE

Four Rabbids walked down a dry, dusty country road.

Suddenly a strange creature appeared. It had a small head, a big butt, and two little legs. And it was covered in feathers!

What was this strange creature?

A hen, of course.

But the Rabbids didn't know that. They had never seen anything like a hen before, so they had no idea what they were seeing. But whatever it was, they thought it was simply hilarious the way it waddled around and bent its head down and pecked at the ground. The Rabbids pointed at the hen and laughed. "BWAHAHAHAHA!"

The hen did not appreciate being laughed at and tried to skitter away. But as you might know, hens don't move very fast. The Rabbids followed the hen, pointing and laughing, down the dusty country road.

Tired of being pointed at and laughed at, the hen let out a frustrated cackle. The cackling sound made the Rabbids laugh even harder. They began cackling themselves.

Then the Rabbids began dancing around to try to imitate the way the hen moved. *Cackle! Laugh!* Point. *Cackle! Laugh!* Point. This crazy dance went on for some time until the Rabbids forgot all about the hen. Seeing her chance to get away, the hen fled toward the henhouse.

## CHAPTER 2:
## RABBIDS RACE

It took a little while for the cackling, dancing Rabbids to realize that the hen wasn't there anymore. But when they did realize that, they were not happy. Where did their toy go? They peered around looking for her and spotted her in the distance.

Three of the Rabbids took off toward the henhouse.

The fourth one, not realizing what had happened, continued to dance and cackle all by himself. *Cackle! Laugh!* Point. Then he realized he was all alone. *Cackle! Laugh! Panic!*

The panicked Rabbid looked around and
spotted his friends in the distance. He
hurried over to the henhouse. When he got
there, he couldn't believe his eyes!

There were *three* of the funny, strange
creatures with big butts! (And yes . . . these
were all hens, but the Rabbids still didn't
know that and let's face it . . . they never
will!) The Rabbids were riding the hens
like broncos and having a race around the
henhouse. It looked like so much fun!

For the Rabbids, anyway. The hens, on
the other hand, did not look very happy.

Feeling left out because he didn't have
his own strange creature to ride, the fourth
Rabbid wandered into the henhouse. He
was sad until he spotted something in the
shadows. Could it be. . . .

# CHAPTER 3:
## WHAT COMES OUT . . .

One of the strange creatures sitting on its big butt, all alone, and waiting to be ridden around the henhouse?

That's exactly what it was! (Well, the part about it being a hen just sitting there is true. The hen was actually *not* hoping to be ridden around the henhouse. She was just trying to relax in the shade.)

The Rabbid walked up to the hen and looked her straight in the eyes.

"Bok?" said the hen.

"Bwahahahaha," said the Rabbid.

"Boooowk! Booowk!" replied the hen.

"BWAHAHAHA!" screamed the Rabbid, terrifying the hen.

And then something amazing happened.
The most wonderful, amazing thing you could ever imagine. (Well, the most amazing thing a Rabbid could ever imagine.) Are you ready? Brace yourself.

Something came out of the creature's
butt. Something smooth and white and
oval-shaped.

*Plop!*

The Rabbid almost fainted from
excitement.

Before now, the Rabbid had no idea that white oval-shaped things could fall out of your butt. Make that *big* white oval-shaped things!

The Rabbid bent over to look at his own butt and imagined being able to make something like that with it. He became even more impressed with this creature, which he still didn't know was a hen.

# CHAPTER 4:
## SPLAT!

Next the Rabbid did the only thing he could think of to do. The most logical thing in the world to do . . . if you are a Rabbid.

He stole the white oval-shaped thing and made a run for it. The Rabbid might not have known what the creature was, but he did know that most creatures don't like having things stolen from them. Especially things they made with their own butts!

The angry hen chased the Rabbid into the yard. After all, she wanted her egg back! The hen caught the Rabbid and pecked him on the back. *Ouch!* Being pecked by a hen doesn't tickle!

The Rabbid fell down and dropped the egg, which went sailing through the air.

And if you have ever dropped an egg, you might know what happened next. That's right. . . .

*Splat!*

The egg landed smack on the back of another Rabbid. The three other Rabbids found this hilarious.

*Cackle! Laugh!* Point.

"BWAHAHAHAHAHA!"

The hen was not amused. In fact, she was furious!

"BOOOOWWK!"

Perhaps it was the sheer exhaustion from chasing the Rabbid to try to get her egg back, or perhaps it was the exhaustion from laying the egg in the first place, but the next thing that happened is that the hen fainted.

The Rabbid was disappointed. *How can more things come out of the creature's butt if it's sleeping?* wondered the Rabbid.

26

The Rabbid decided to go find another creature with a big butt. He didn't have to look very hard. (It was, after all, a henhouse.)

"Bok?" said the hen.

"Bwahh!" said the Rabbid.

"Bok bok?" asked the hen.

"Bwaaah BWAAAH!" screamed the Rabbid, remembering what happened last time. And the oval-shaped thing fell out of the creature's butt again.

*So that's how it works,* thought the Rabbid, who stole this egg too and ran into the yard.

If I asked you what the Rabbid was going to do next, what would you say?

If you said, "The Rabbid is going to chuck the egg at another Rabbid and start an egg war!" then you would be correct!

That's just what the Rabbid did.

The other Rabbid ran into the henhouse to grab his own creature that makes oval-shaped things come out of its butt (in other words, his own hen.) The two Rabbids fired eggs back and forth at each other.

Their weapon of choice? Hen butts.

Their ammunition? Eggs.

One, two, three, four, Rabbids declare an egg war!

# CHAPTER 5:
# ARE YOU MY MOTHER?

This egg war would have gone on all day,
or at least until the hens ran out of eggs,
but something happened that changed
everything. One of the eggs hit a Rabbid,
but instead of gooey, slimy yolk pouring out,
an adorable little yellow chick popped out.

The stunned Rabbids stopped firing eggs
for a moment and stared at the strange little
creature.

The baby chick looked at the Rabbid it landed on, and, being only a few seconds old, got confused and thought the Rabbid was his mother. He tried to snuggle up to the Rabbid, which was actually really cute and adorable, but the Rabbid got annoyed and pushed it away. . . .

But the chick came right back to his Rabbid-mommy. (Those baby chicks are as persistent as they are cute!)

Not many creatures can resist a cute and adorable baby chick . . . but a Rabbid can. Annoyed, the Rabbid tried to walk away from the chick. The chick, maybe thinking his mommy was playing a game, just followed.

Now the Rabbid was *really* annoyed. He picked up the chick and was about to toss it out of his way when suddenly a dark shadow fell across the yard.

The Rabbid looked up and saw . . .

# CHAPTER 6:
# RUN!

The rooster. (Also known as the baby chick's daddy.)

The rooster was huge . . . and angry. He let out a mighty yell.

The Rabbid realized he might be in *big* trouble, so he did something that he thought was a very good idea. (If you've been following along closely, you might know even before you turn the page that this idea probably isn't very good at all.)

Do you really want to know what the Rabbid did next? Think of what you might do (run?) and then think of what you would never, ever do. That's what the Rabbid did.

37

The Rabbid took the chick, placed it back inside the broken eggshell and then placed it back inside the hen's butt as if to say "Nothing to see here!" to the big angry rooster.

"BOK?" yelled the hen.

Amazingly, the rooster calmed down. Or maybe he was just confused. The Rabbids realized that now would be the perfect time to escape, and so they whistled as they calmly strolled out of the yard, away from the henhouse.

Nothing to see here! Nothing at all!

As soon as they reached the road, the Rabbids took off running as fast as they could. They wanted to get as far away from the henhouse as possible. But then one of the Rabbids stopped running and screeched to a halt. The other Rabbids stopped too.

What caught the Rabbid's attention?

In a field, next to the road, stood a *humongous* creature with brown spots. It had an even bigger butt than the creatures in the henhouse did, and instead of saying "Bok!" it said "Moo!"

The creature, of course, was a cow. But the Rabbids didn't know that. (And let's face it . . . they never will!) They also didn't know that the stuff falling out of the cow's butt wasn't eggs.

They were about to find out exactly what it was. And it was a lesson they would never forget.